CONTENTS

Glossary

 **assist** a pass to a teammate in a way that leads to a score

 **basket** the net and the metal ring it hangs from at each end of a basketball court

 **dribble** to bounce the ball non-stop with one hand while walking or running down the court

 **lay-up** a one-handed shot made near the basket, usually off the backboard

 **point guard** the player who controls the ball and makes sure it gets to the right player at the right time

Chapter 1
SIGN ME UP!

Gregory heard a noise outside. He looked out of his window. His older brother, Quincy, was playing basketball with some friends. Gregory went outside. He loved to watch his brother shoot baskets.

Quincy saw Gregory and smiled. "Take a shot, little brother," he said. He handed Gregory the ball.

Gregory pretended he was in a big game. He thought about a crowd of people cheering for him. He counted down in his head. *Three . . . two . . . one!*

He shot the ball. It went through the basket perfectly. *SWISH!* Gregory jumped up and down. "Yes!" he cried.

"Well done!" Quincy said. He gave
Gregory a high-five. So did Quincy's
friends.

"I love basketball," Gregory said. "One
day I want to be a famous player. I want
to be on TV!"

Quincy patted Gregory's head. "You need to grow a bit first," he said. "You have a lot to learn about the game too. Do you even know what different players do? Do you know the rules?"

Gregory shook his head. "I don't need to know that stuff," he said. "I'm just going to make all the shots and be the star!"

"Well, there's a basketball club for kids your age," Quincy said. "Would you like to join?"

Gregory grinned. "Yes!" he said.

"Let's ask Mum and Dad to sign you up," Quincy said. "Remember, basketball is a team sport. It's not about just one player. You need your buddies."

But Gregory wasn't listening. He was shooting basket after basket. *SWISH! SWISH! SWISH!*

Chapter 2
PRACTICE PROBLEMS

It was the first day of basketball practice. Gregory walked into the gym and saw a group of kids. A loud whistle blew.

"OK, line up!" a tall woman shouted. "My name is Mrs Miller. I'm the coach. We're going to have a lot of fun learning to play basketball. First, let's tell everyone our names."

Gregory stepped forward. "I'm Gregory. I'm going to be the team's best player," he said.

The girl next to Gregory spoke next. "My name is Simone. And *I'm* going to be the team's best player," she said.

Gregory and Simone turned to look at each other. Neither one of them blinked.

Coach Miller laughed. "We'll see," she said. "We have to work together to win. Let's start with passing drills."

She paired up the kids and gave each pair a basketball. Gregory and Simone were partners. Gregory made a perfect bounce pass to Simone. Her return pass shot off to the side.

The partners spent some time passing.
Gregory was happy. He was doing well.
He passed the ball much better than
Simone. After passing drills were finished,
the kids practised shooting.

Towards the end of practice, Coach Miller blew her whistle again. She split the kids into two teams. "Now let's have a little practice game," she said.

Gregory and Simone both pumped their fists. They were on different teams. Gregory's team would try to score a goal first.

"I've got this!" Gregory told his teammates. He grabbed the ball and dribbled down the court. He went fast. He was going to score!

Gregory shot the ball. But he didn't see
Byron standing by the basket. Byron was
on the other team. He was tall. *THWACCKK!*
He blocked Gregory's shot.

Gregory grabbed the ball and tried again. This time, three other kids were in his way. The ball bounced off his foot.

Simone snatched the ball and took off towards the other basket. Gregory watched as she easily scored a goal for her team.

Chapter 3
HELPING HANDS

Gregory was upset with himself. He wasn't playing well. He walked off the court, shaking his head.

"Everyone, stop!" Coach Miller said. "What's wrong, Gregory?"

"I want to shoot for the points, like the players on TV," Gregory said. "But I keep messing up."

Coach Miller walked over and put her hand on Gregory's shoulder. "Basketball is about sharing," she said. "Every player has a job to do. Five players must work as one to win."

Gregory nodded. "I know," he said quietly.

"We all bring something special to the game," Coach Miller said. "You are a great passer, Gregory. I think you would make a perfect point guard."

Gregory wrinkled his nose. "What's that?" he asked.

"Point guards help lead the charge," Coach Miller said. "They look for teammates who are open and can take a shot. Then they make a pass to them. That's called an assist."

She handed Gregory the ball. "Try it," she said.

Coach Miller called everyone to their spots. Gregory started to go for the basket, but then he stopped. He looked up and saw Alex. She had her hands up in the air. She was free! He passed the ball to her. She caught it and made a lay-up. *SWISH!* Goal!

"Perfect! Let's try another assist," Coach Miller said.

Gregory dribbled to the basket again. This time he saw the other team coming. He passed the ball to Tim, and Tim made an easy shot! Gregory and his teammates cheered.

"That's how we do it!" Coach Miller said. "Great play, Gregory. Working together makes the game easier."

Gregory smiled. "My brother said you need your buddies in basketball. I guess he was right!"

HOT POTATO PASSING

Passing is an important skill in basketball. Making a good pass can help move the ball down the court. It can also help your teammates score goals.

Grab a friend and play this fun passing game! Move the ball out of your hands quickly, as if it were a hot potato. And don't throw the ball too hard. A good pass should be easy for your teammate to catch.

What you need:
- an area with space for passing
- a basketball

What you do:
1. Holding the ball, stand across from your friend.
2. Say "Bounce pass!" and try to pass the ball to your friend with one bounce. Pass the ball back and forth for 30 seconds.
3. Next, say "Chest pass!" Using two hands, pass the ball from your chest to your friend's chest. Pass the ball back and forth for 30 seconds.
4. Next, say "Overhead pass!" Using two hands raised just above your head, pass the ball to your friend. Pass back and forth for 30 seconds.
5. Finally, call out the passes in any order. Think fast!

REPLAY IT

Have another look at this illustration. Gregory was upset with himself. He didn't feel like he'd played his best. How did Coach Miller show Gregory she cared about him?

Now pretend you are Gregory. Write a thank-you e-mail to Coach Miller. Tell her about the skills you learned during practice, including how to be a better team player.

ABOUT THE AUTHOR

Elliott Smith is a former sports reporter who covered athletes in all sports. He is one of the authors of the Natural Thrills series about extreme outdoor sports. In his spare time, he likes playing sport with his two children and going to the cinema.

ABOUT
THE ILLUSTRATOR

Katie Kear is a graduate of the University of Gloucestershire, with a degree in illustration. Reading has always played an important part in Katie's life, and it was her deep love for books that made her choose a career in illustration. When she's not drawing, Katie enjoys adventures in nature, chocolate, stationery, the smell of cherries and finding new artists to inspire her.